WE'RE GOING ON A GINGERBREAD HUNT

WRITTEN BY **ANNA MEMBRINO**

ILLUSTRATED BY **GLADYS JOSE**

Cartwheel Books
An imprint of Scholastic Inc.
New York

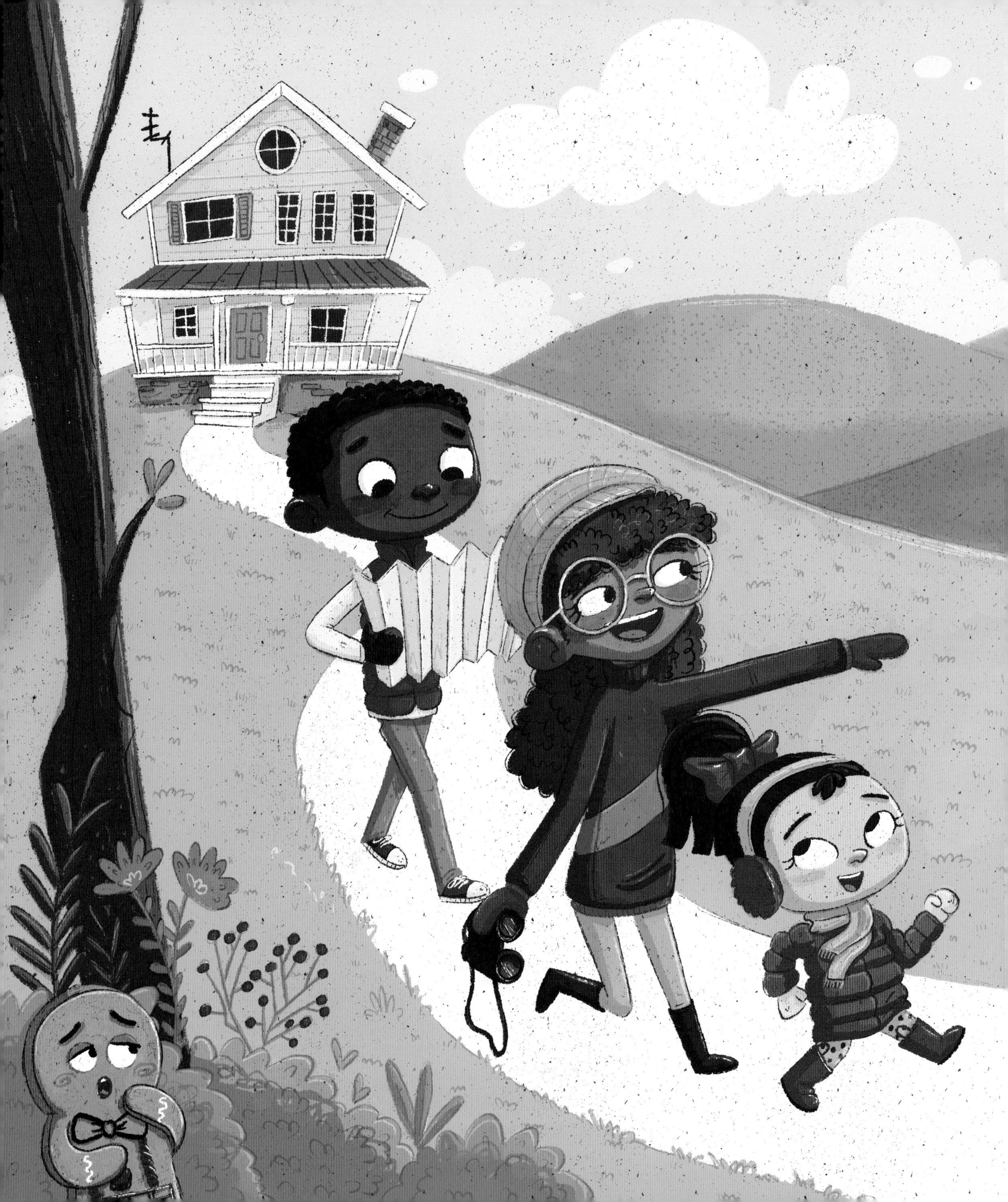

We're going on a gingerbread hunt!
We're going on a gingerbread hunt!

We're going to eat
a big one.

HERE WE
COME!

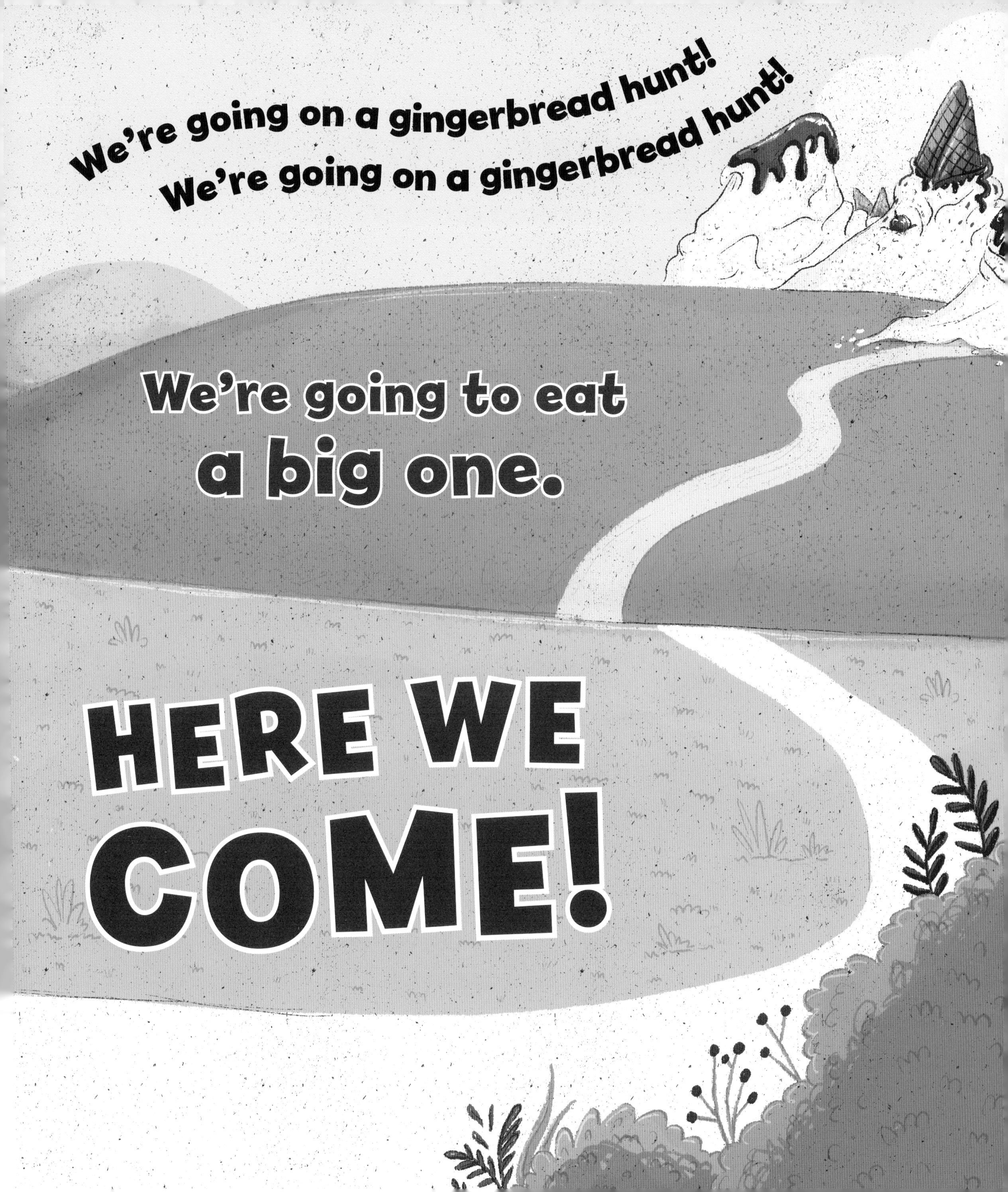

OH LOOK!

A sticky ice cream glacier.

We can't go over it.
We can't go under it.
We've got to ride through it!

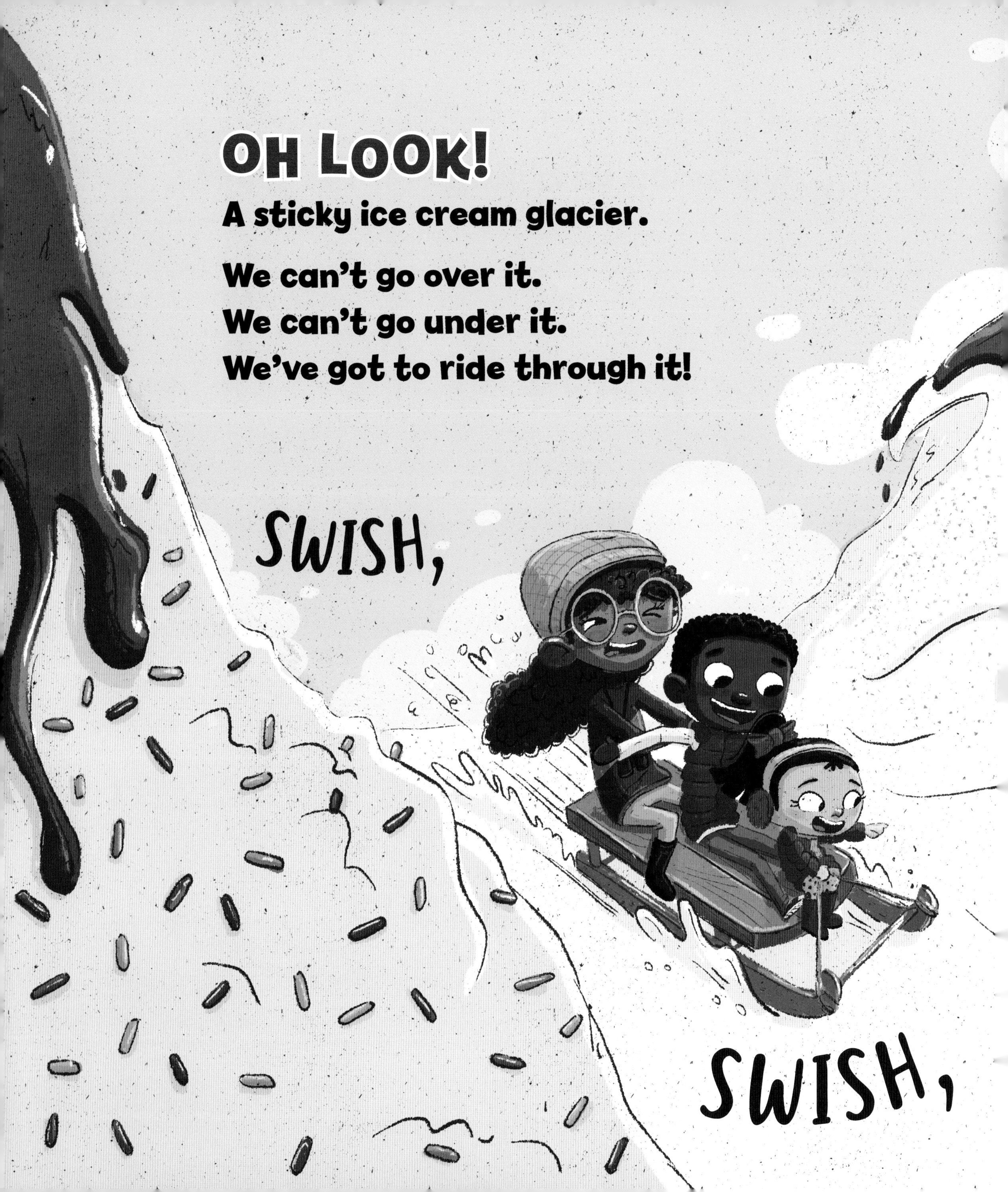

SWISH,

SWISH,

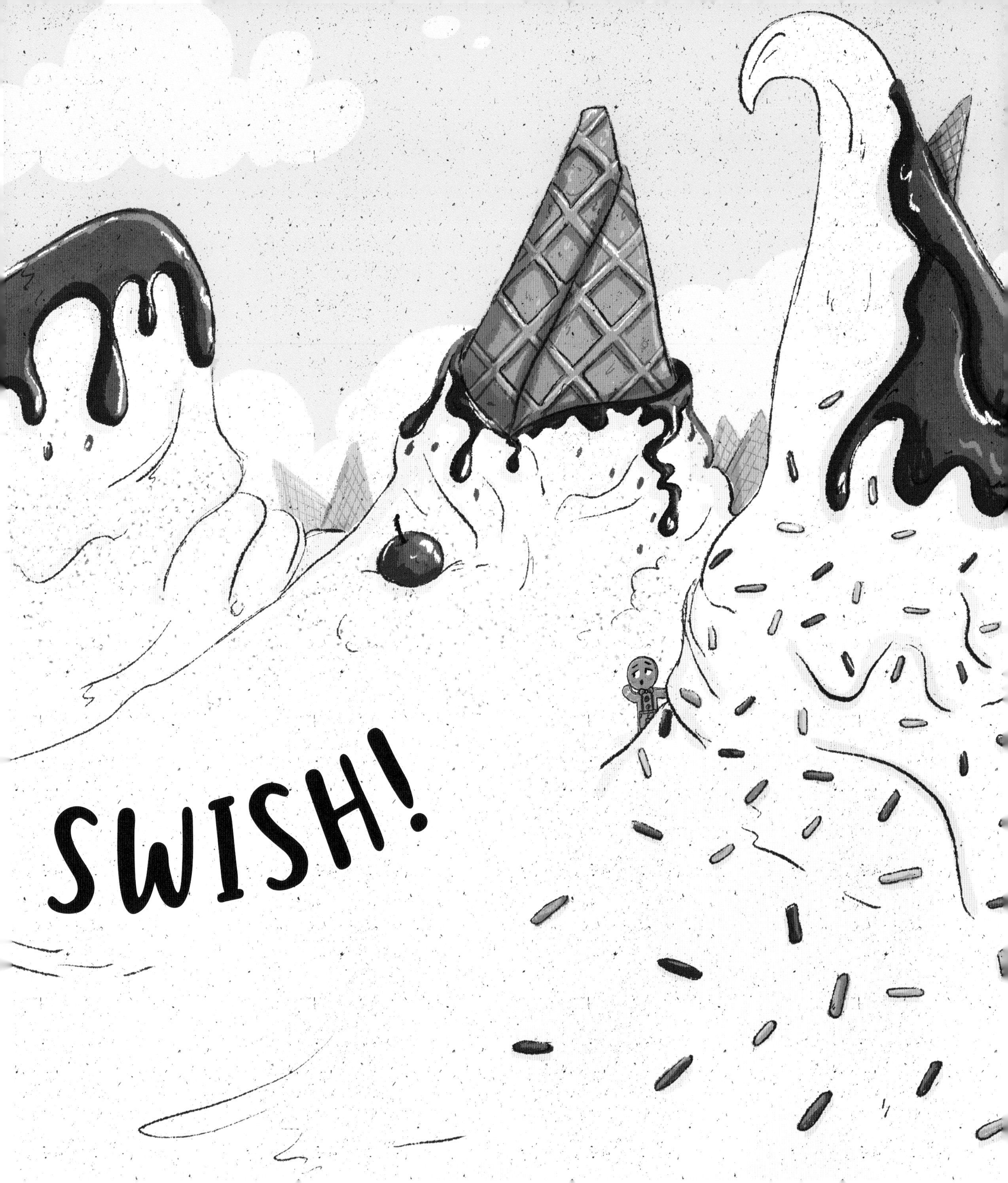
SWISH!

We're going on a gingerbread hunt!
We're going on a gingerbread hunt!

We're going to eat
a big one.

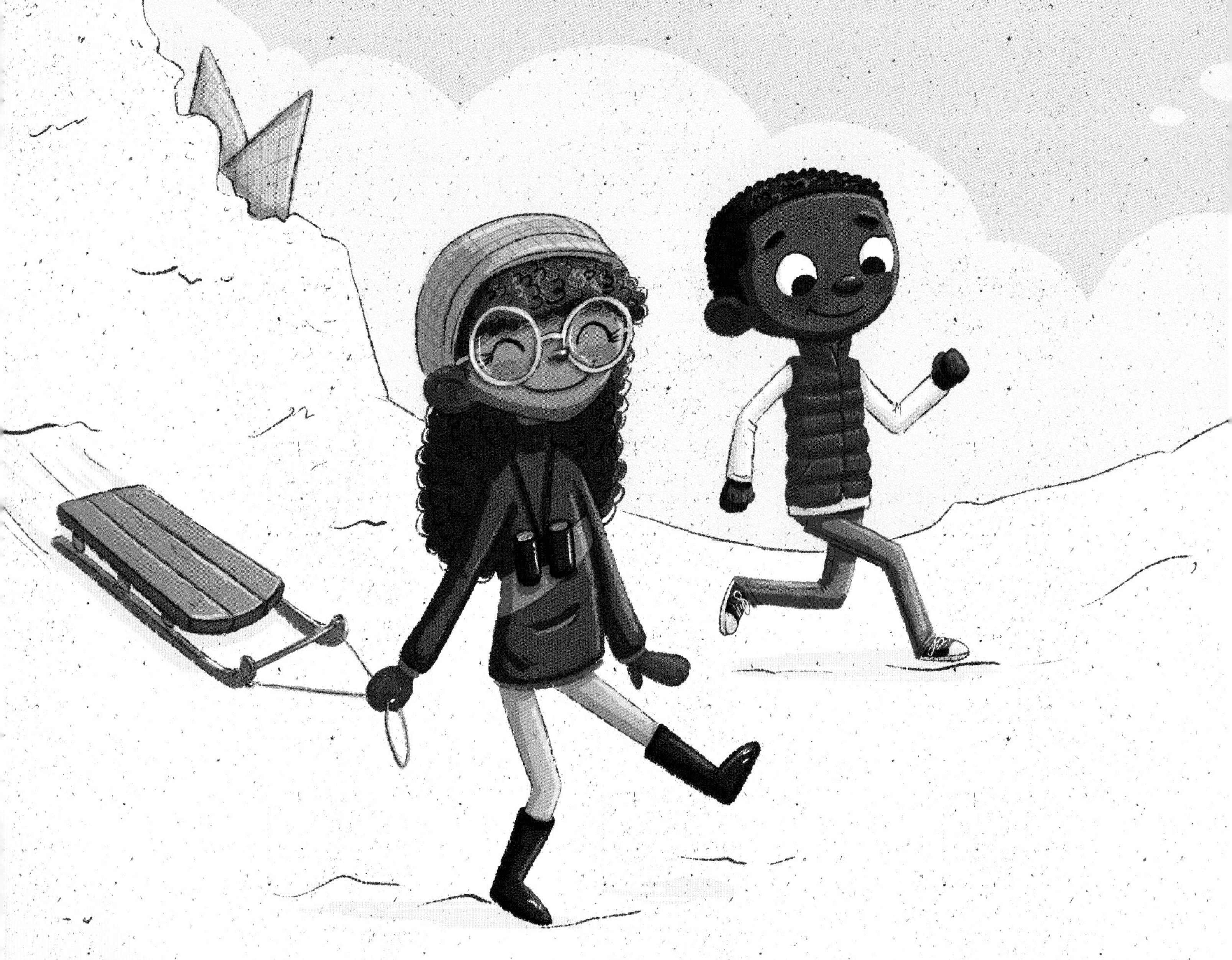

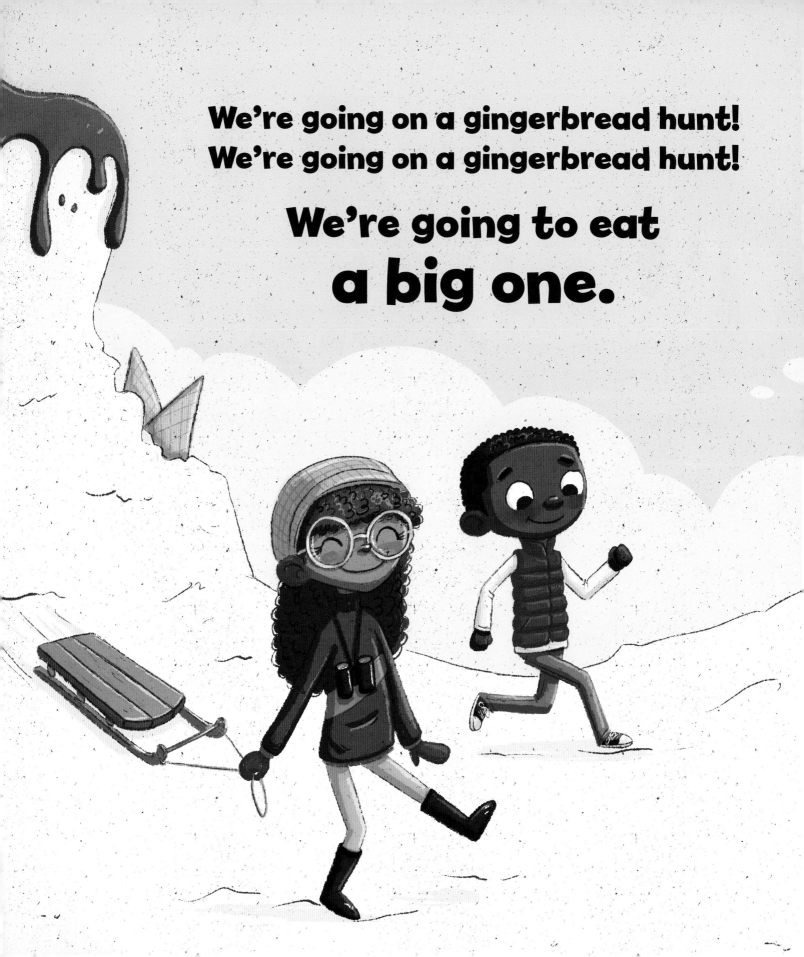

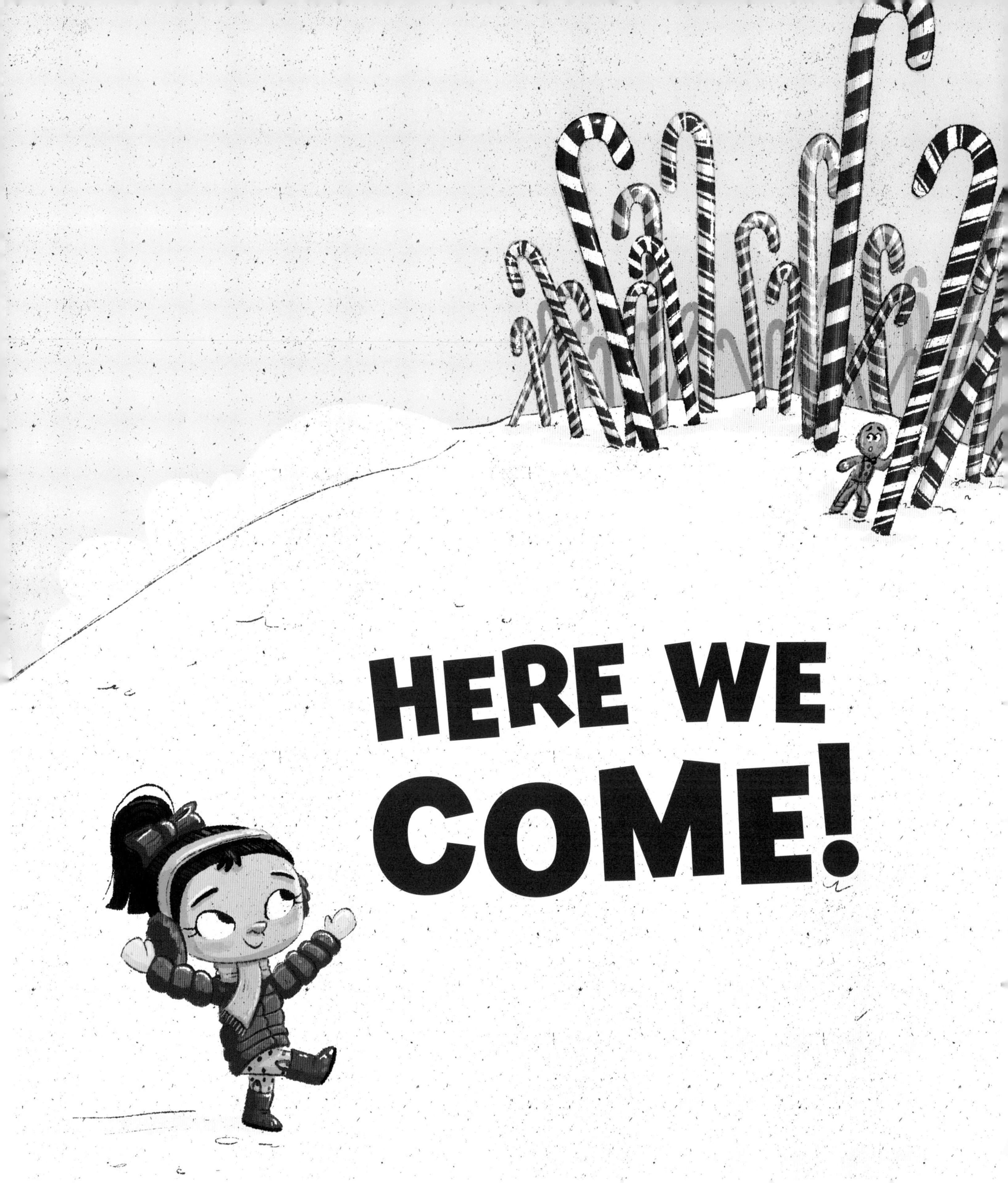

HERE WE COME!

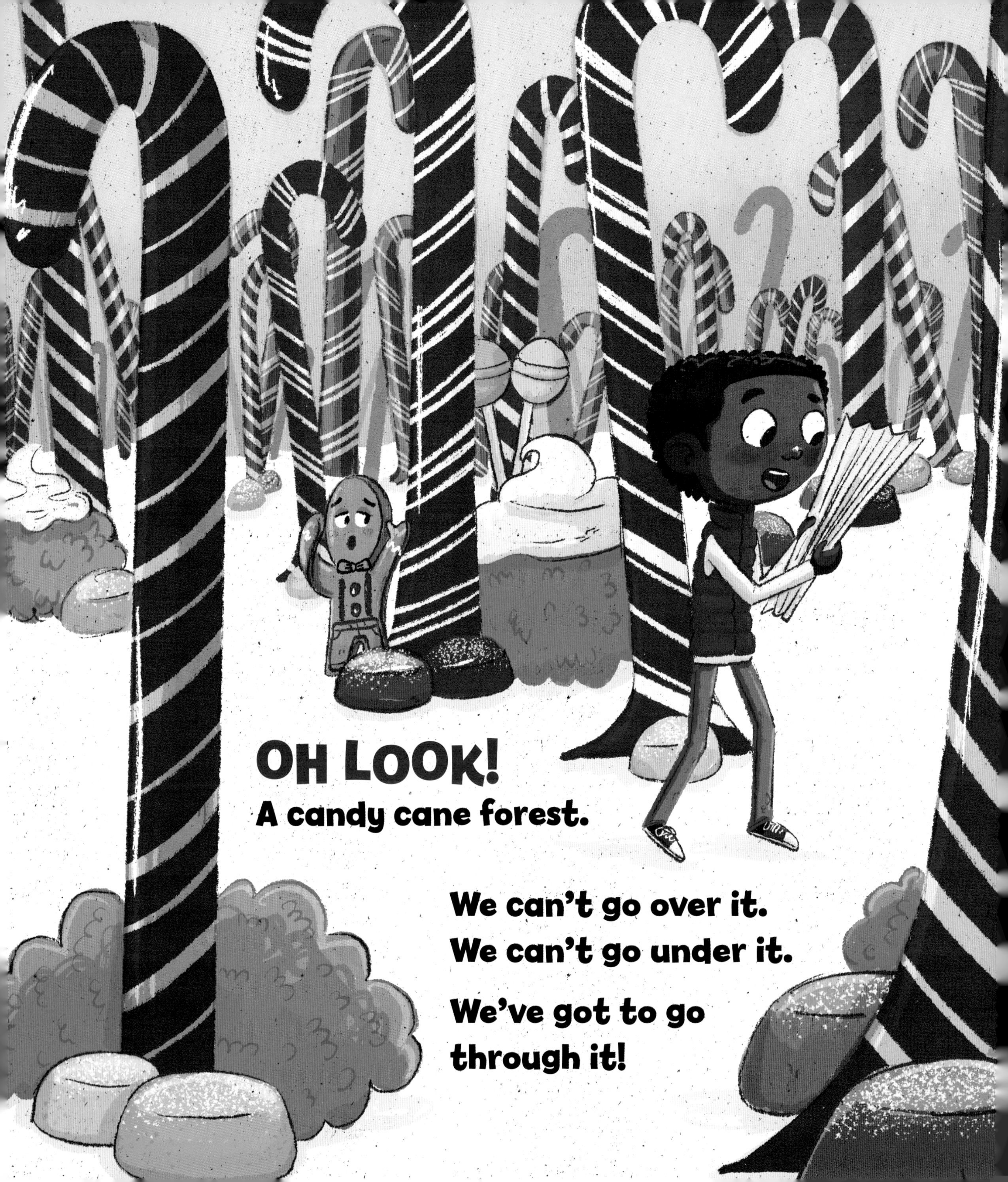

OH LOOK!
A candy cane forest.

We can't go over it.
We can't go under it.

We've got to go through it!

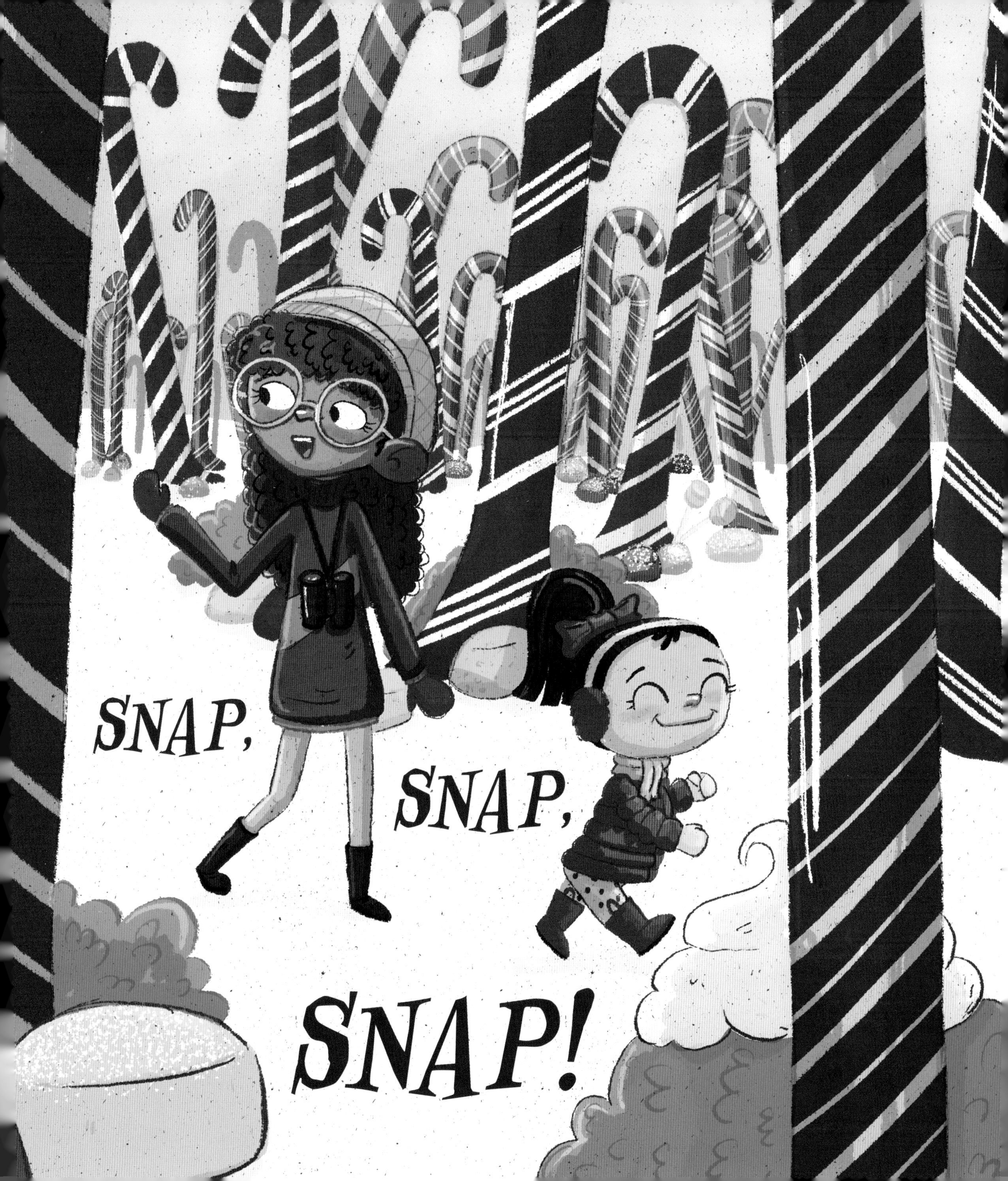

SNAP,

SNAP,

SNAP!

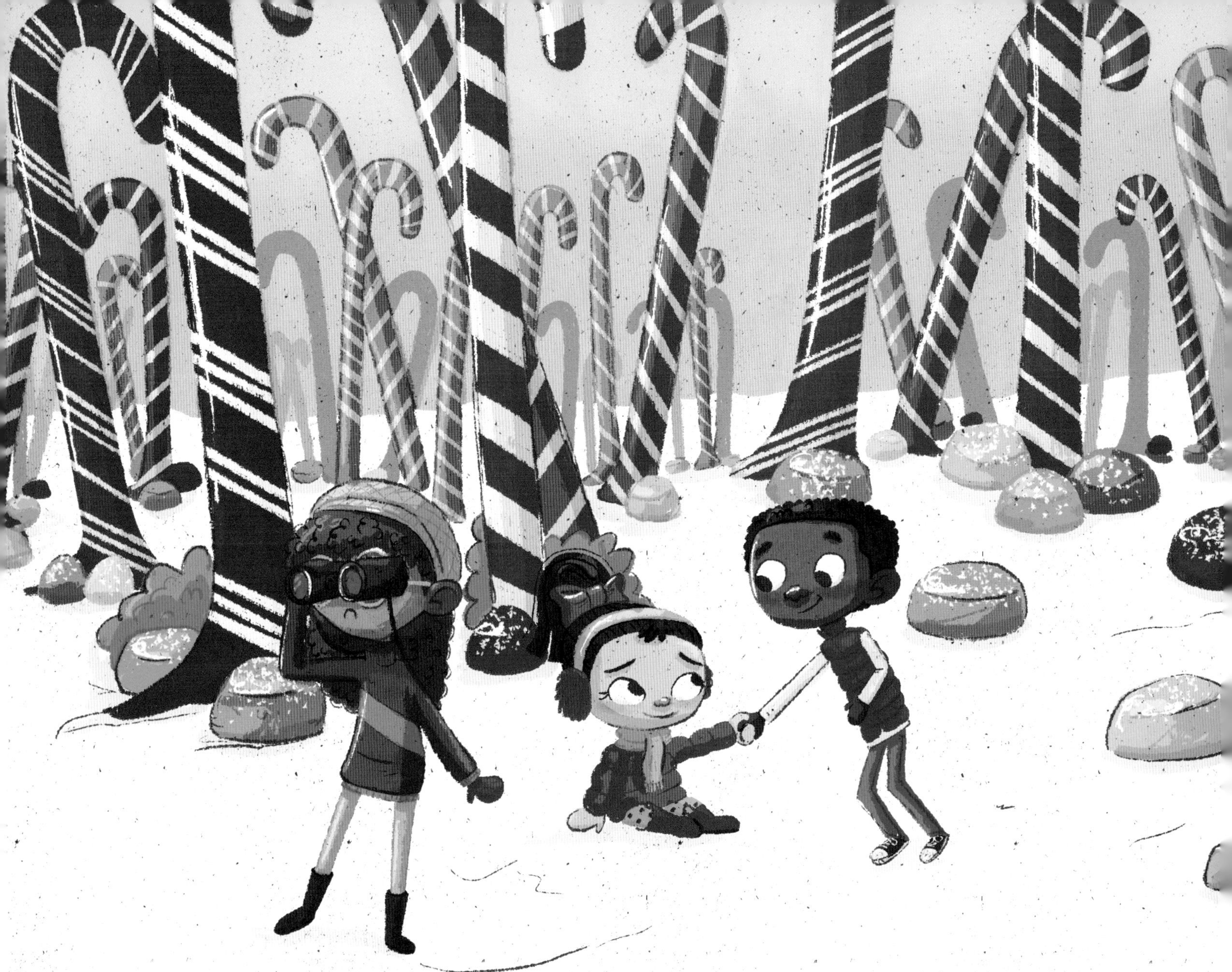

We're going on a gingerbread hunt!
We're going on a gingerbread hunt!

We're going to eat
a big one!

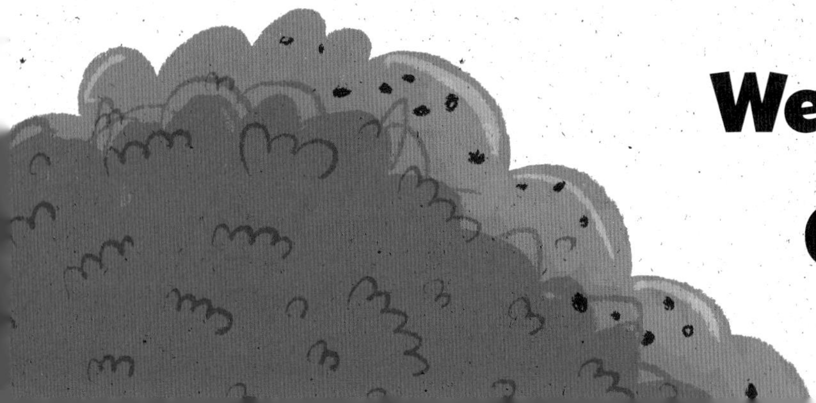

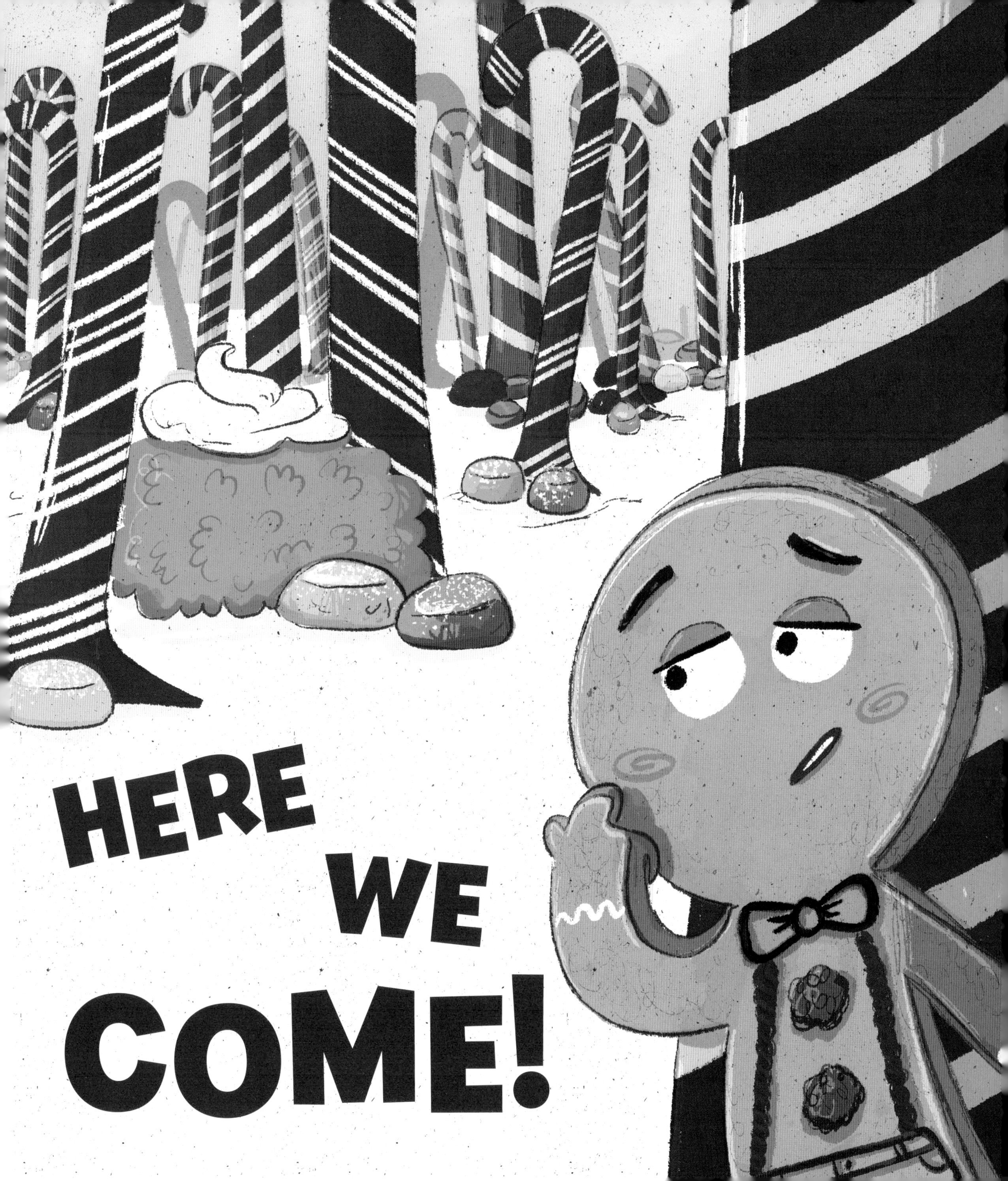

HERE WE COME!

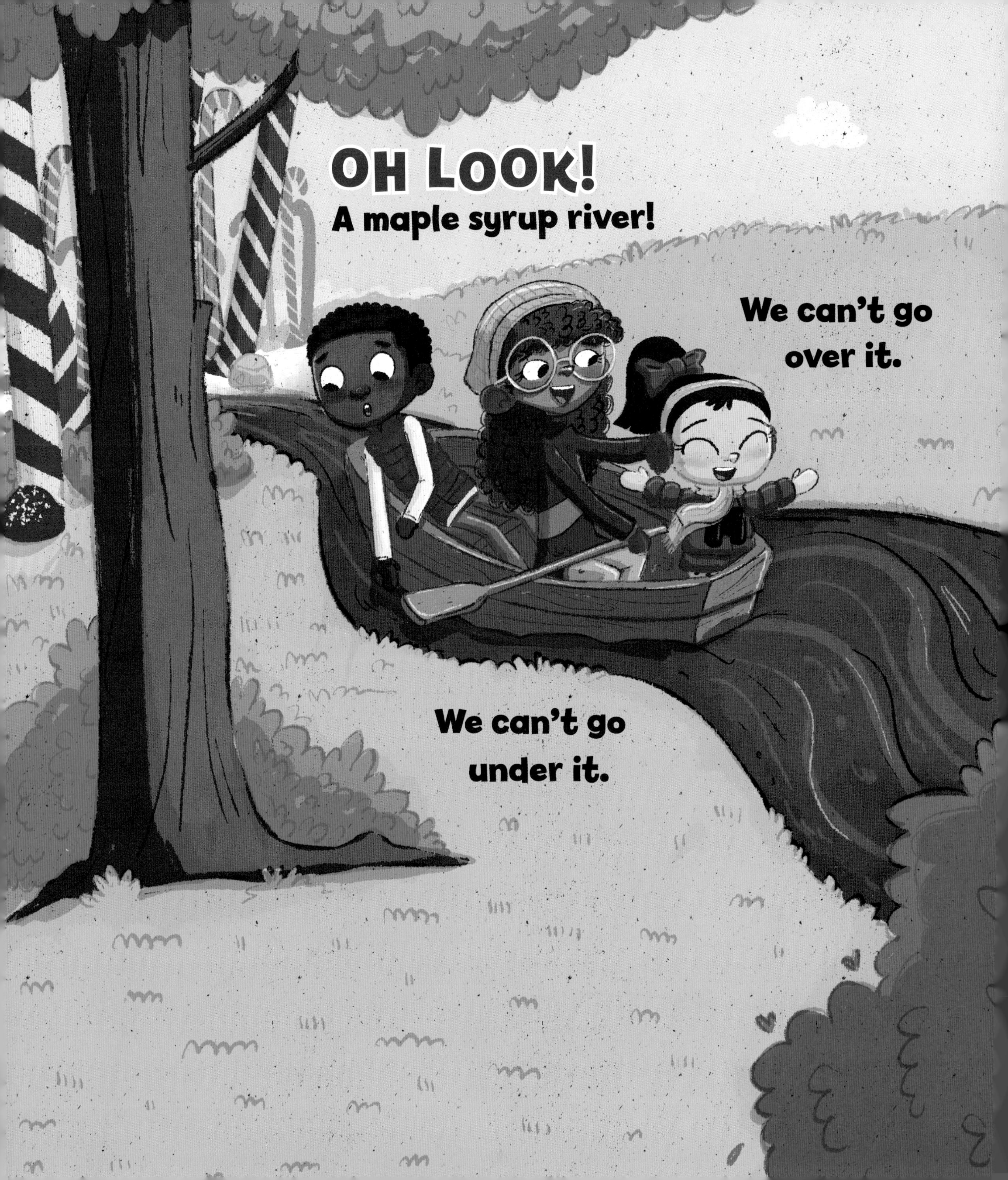

OH LOOK!
A maple syrup river!

We can't go over it.

We can't go under it.

We've got
to ride
through it!

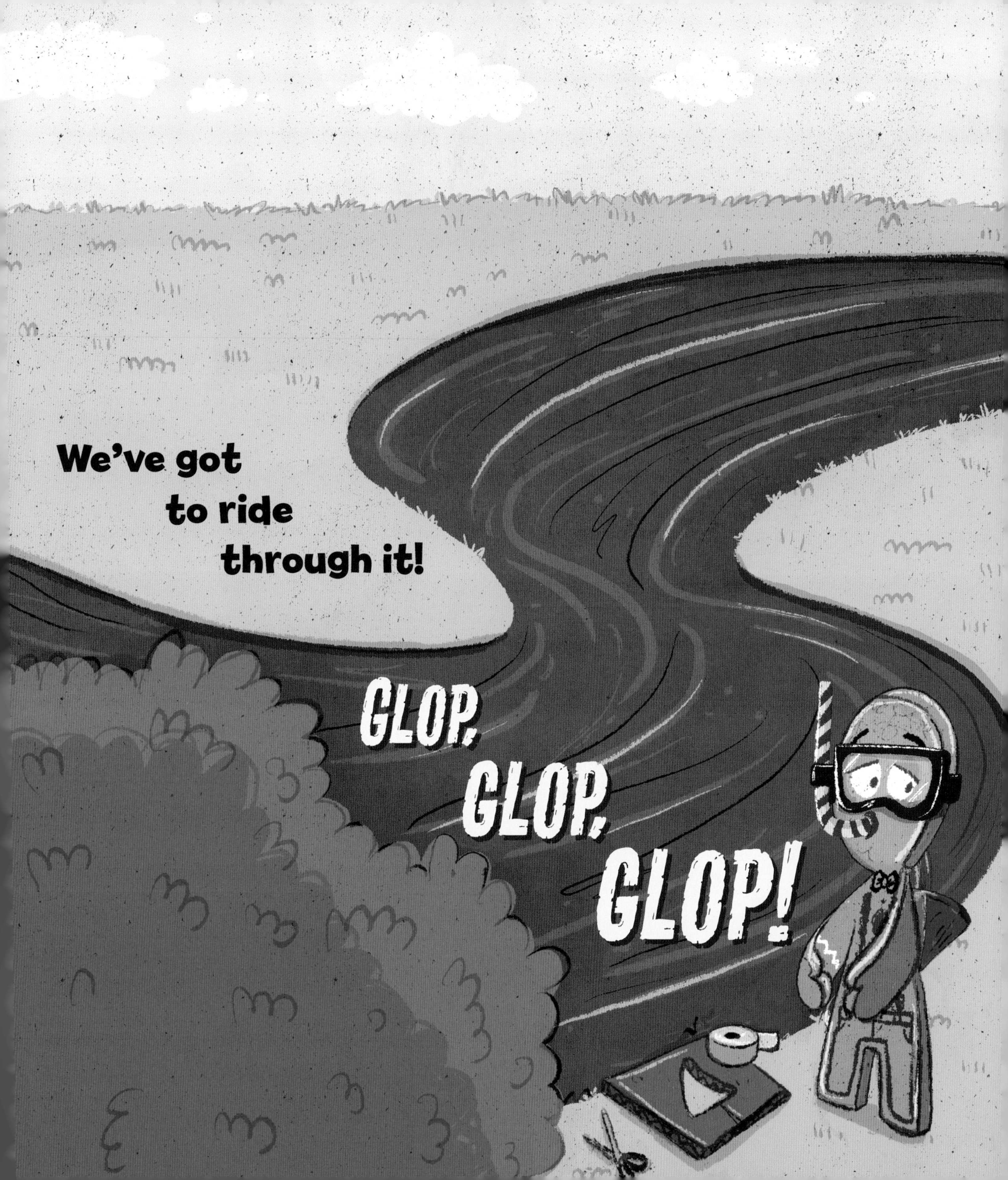

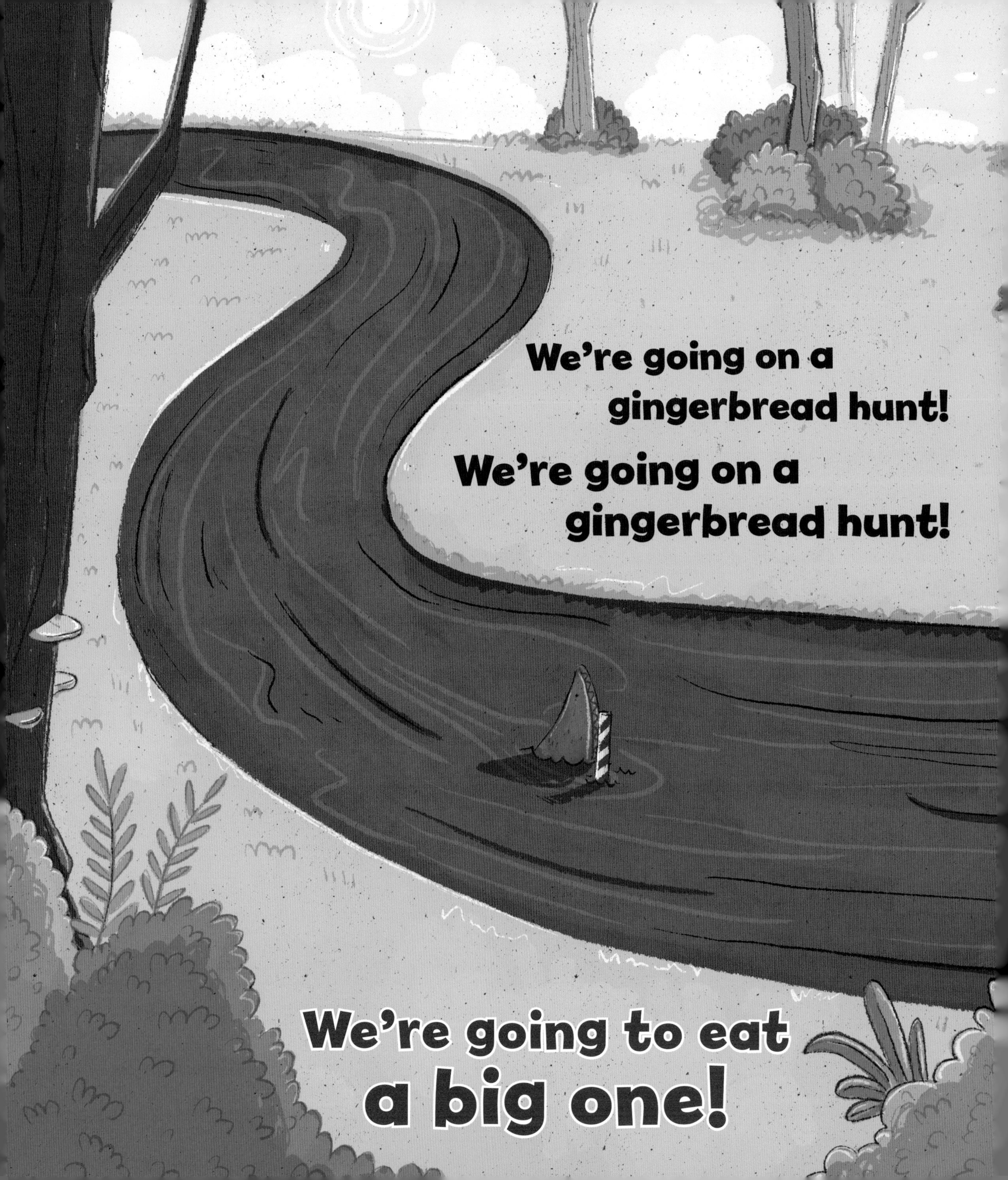

We're going on a
gingerbread hunt!
We're going on a
gingerbread hunt!

We're going to eat
a big one!

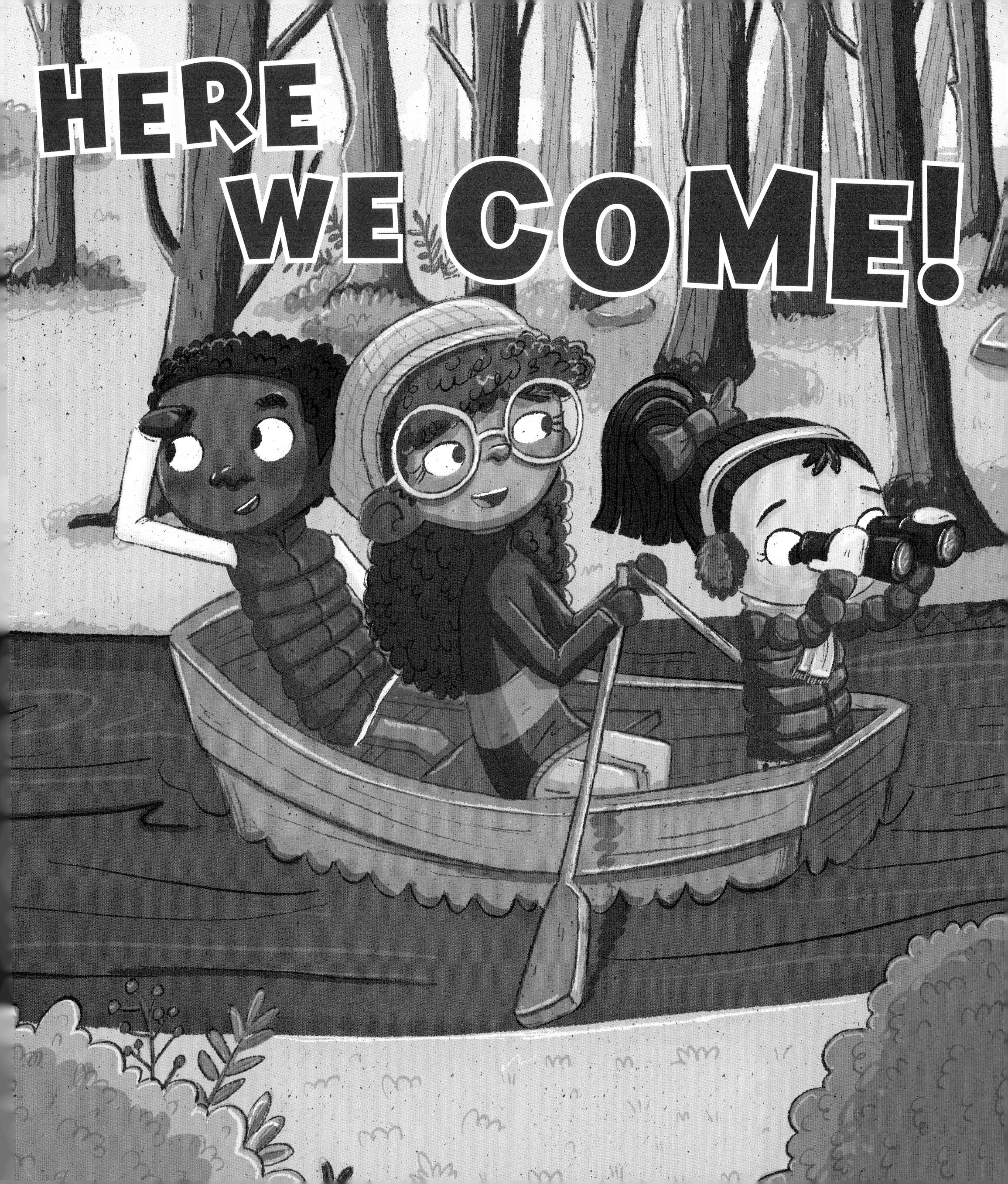
HERE WE COME!

OH LOOK!

A salty pretzel cave!

We can't go over it.
We can't go under it.
We've got to go through it!

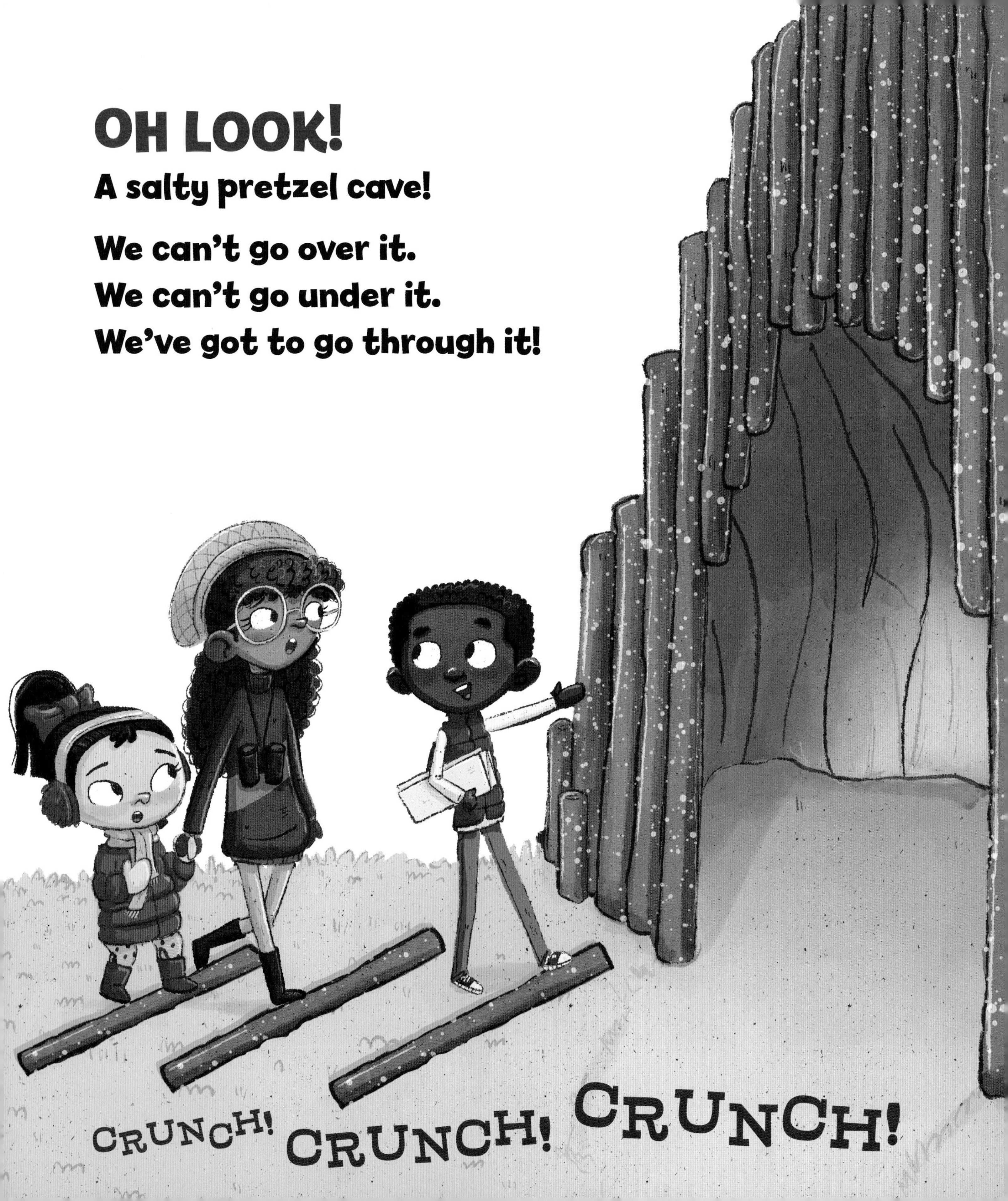

CRUNCH! CRUNCH! CRUNCH!

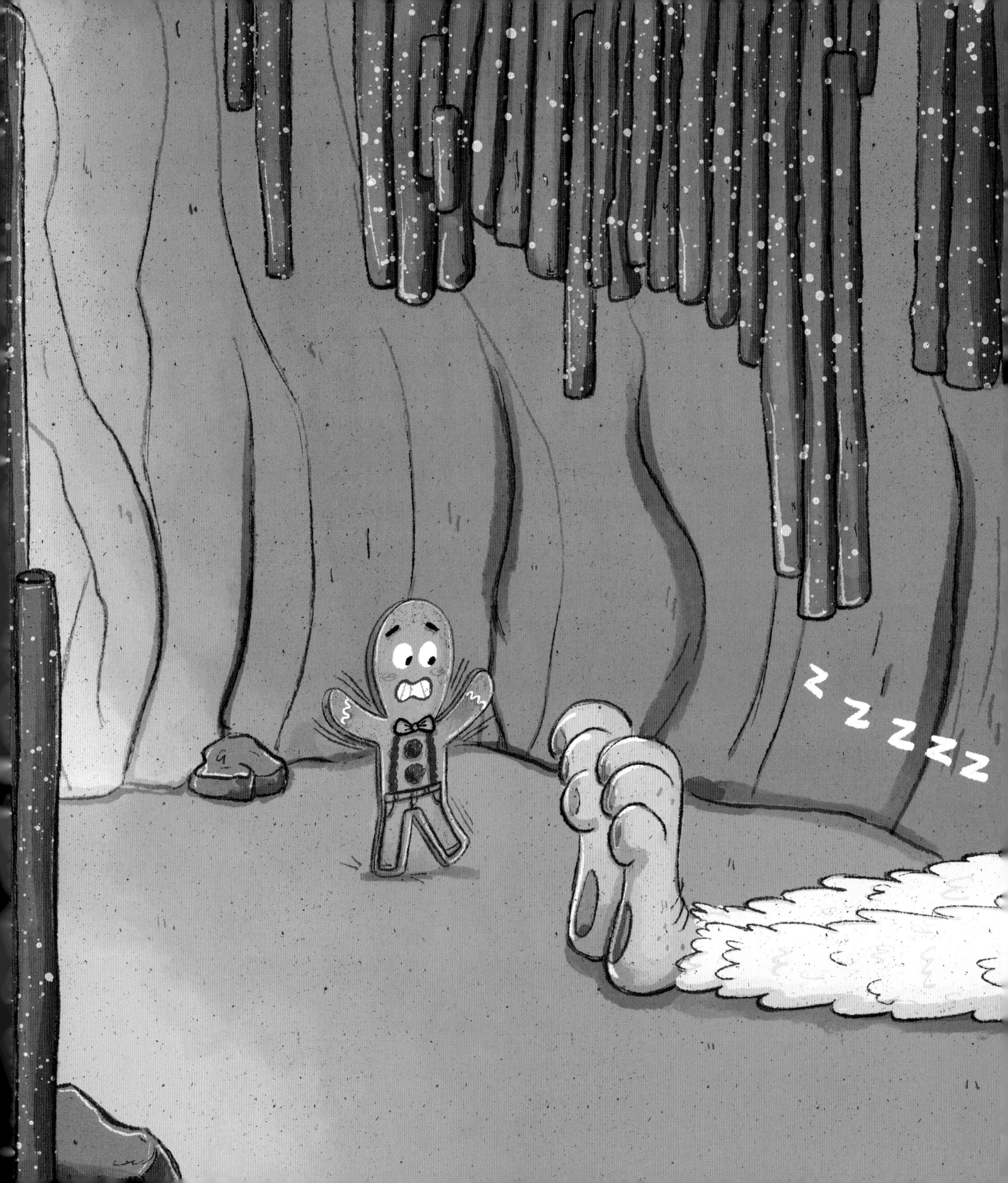
Z Z Z Z Z

WHAT'S THAT?

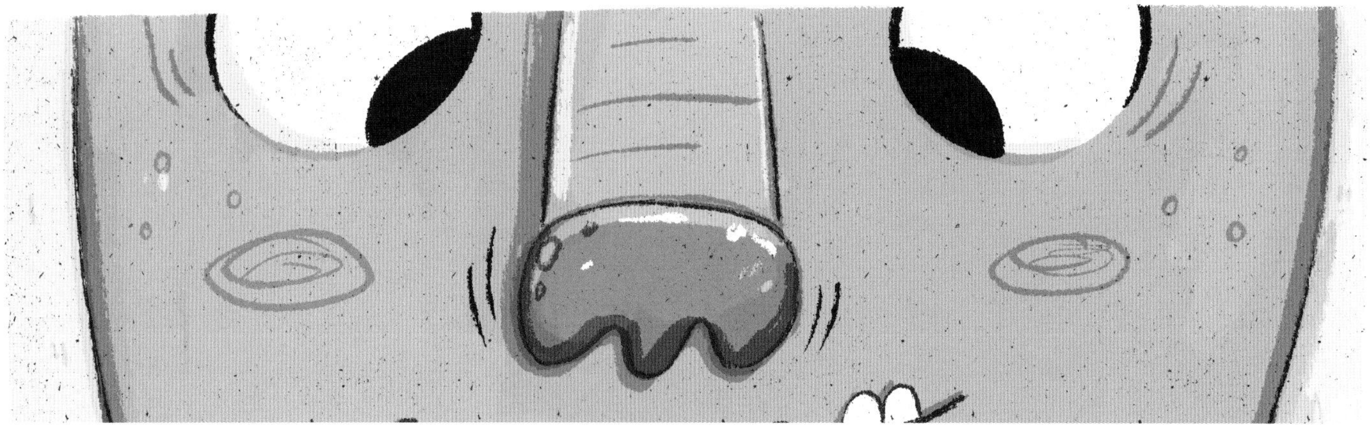

One shiny wet nose!

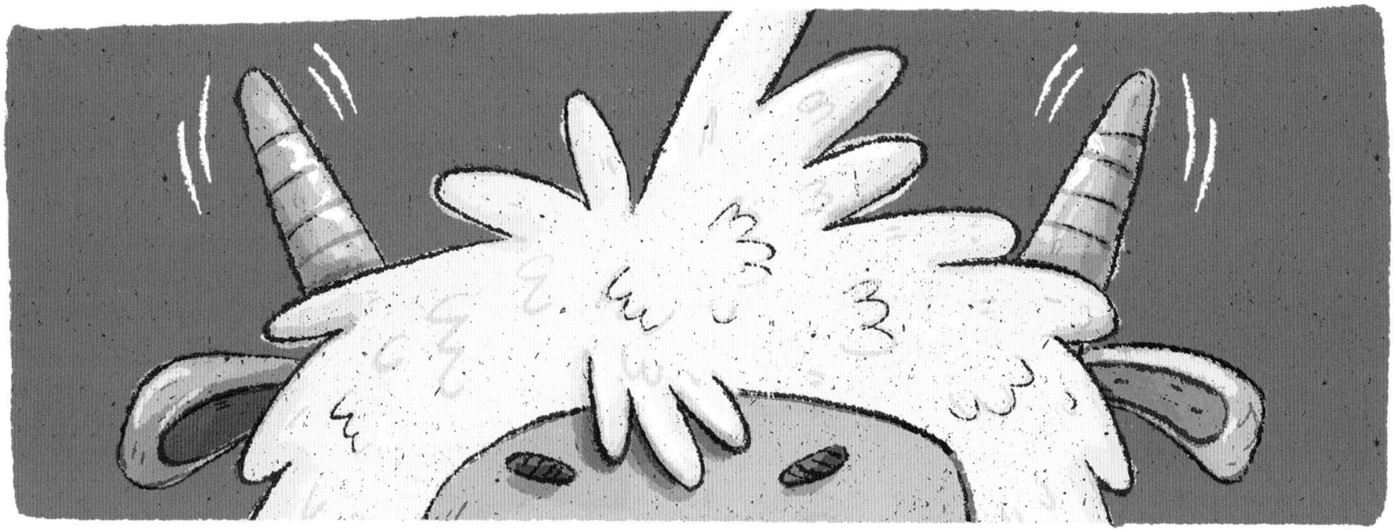

Two shiny gold horns!

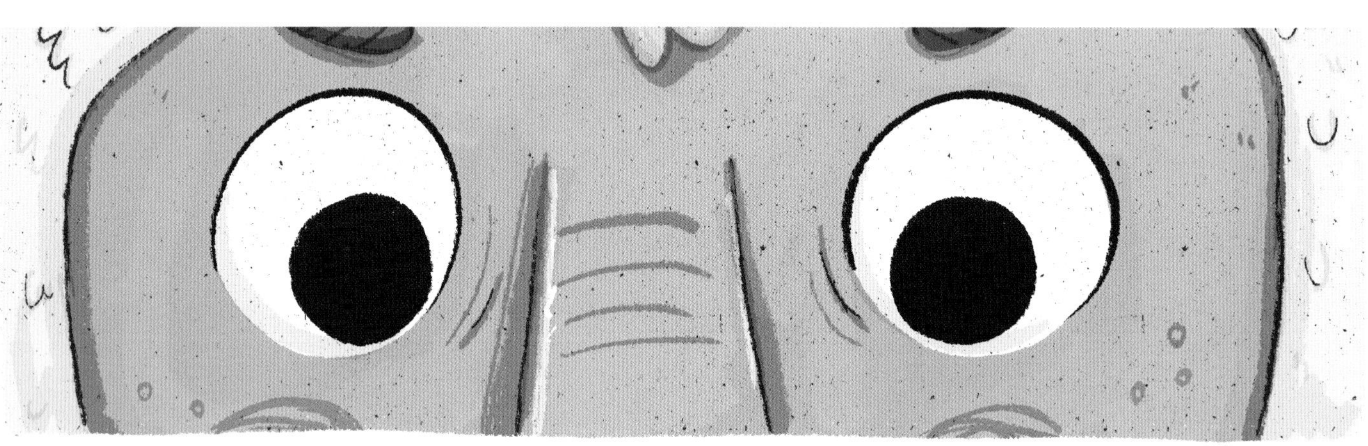

Two big googly eyes!

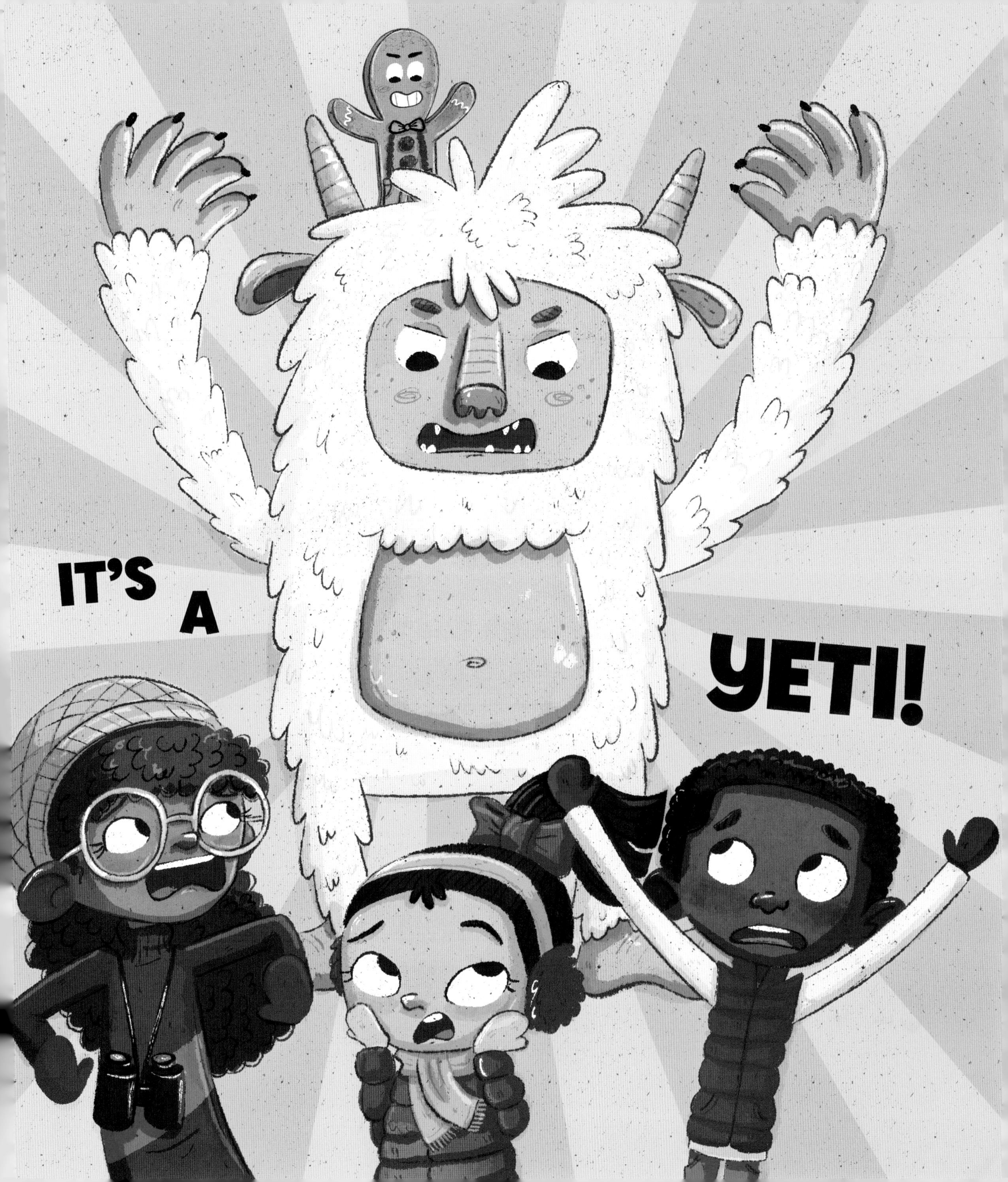

IT'S A YETI!

QUICK!

Back through the cave!

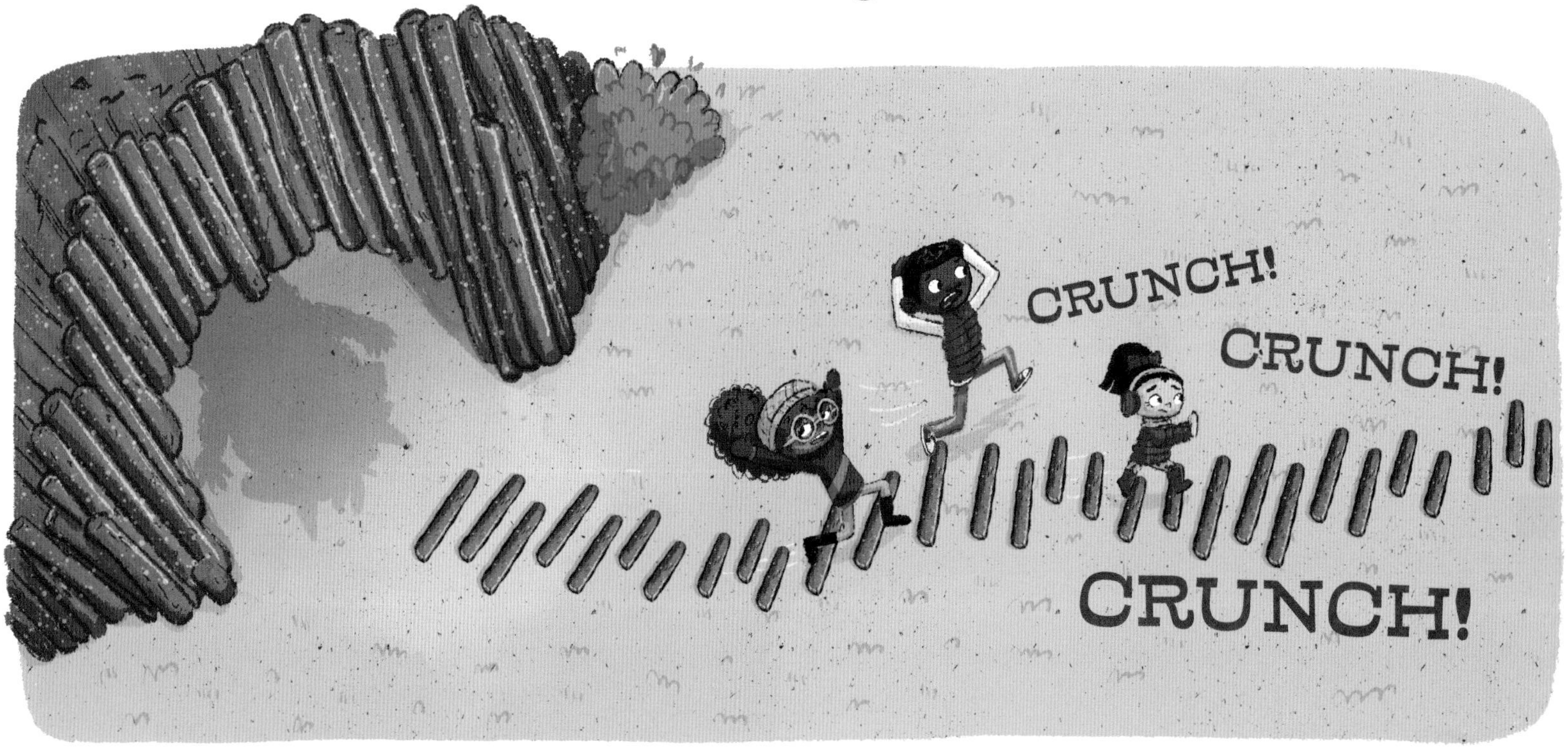
CRUNCH!
CRUNCH!
CRUNCH!

Back through the river!

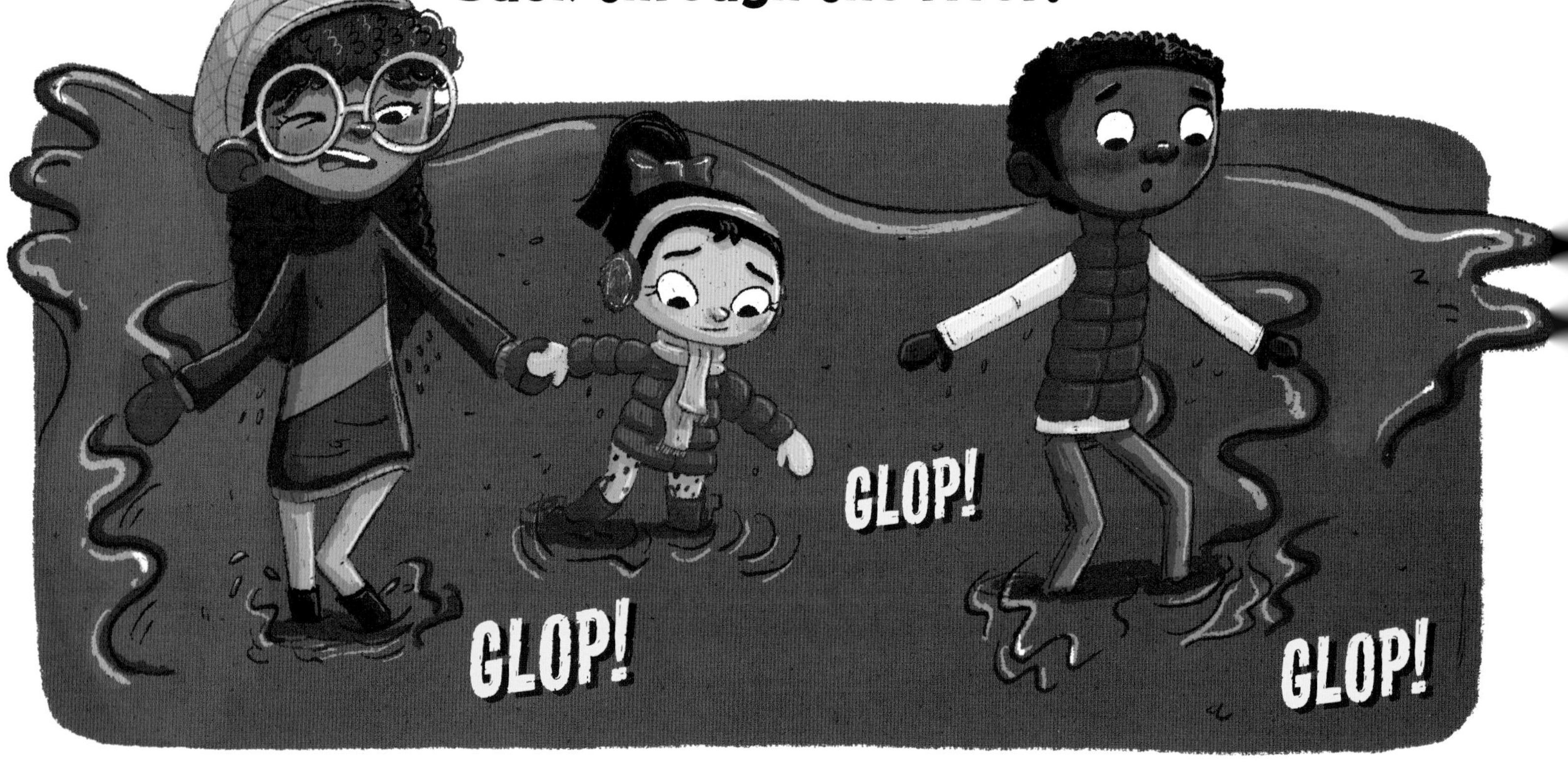
GLOP!
GLOP!
GLOP!

Back through the forest!

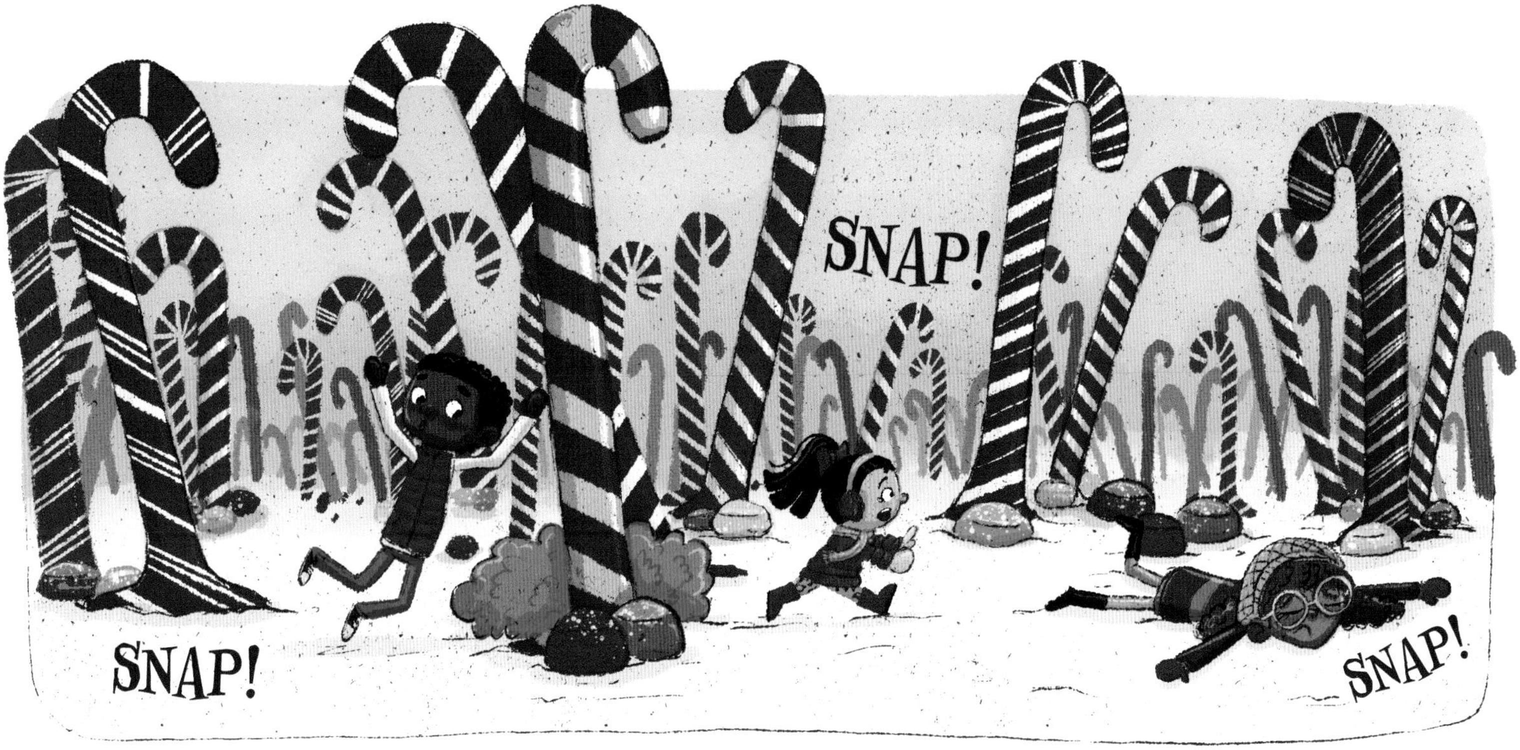
SNAP!
SNAP!
SNAP!

Back through the glacier!

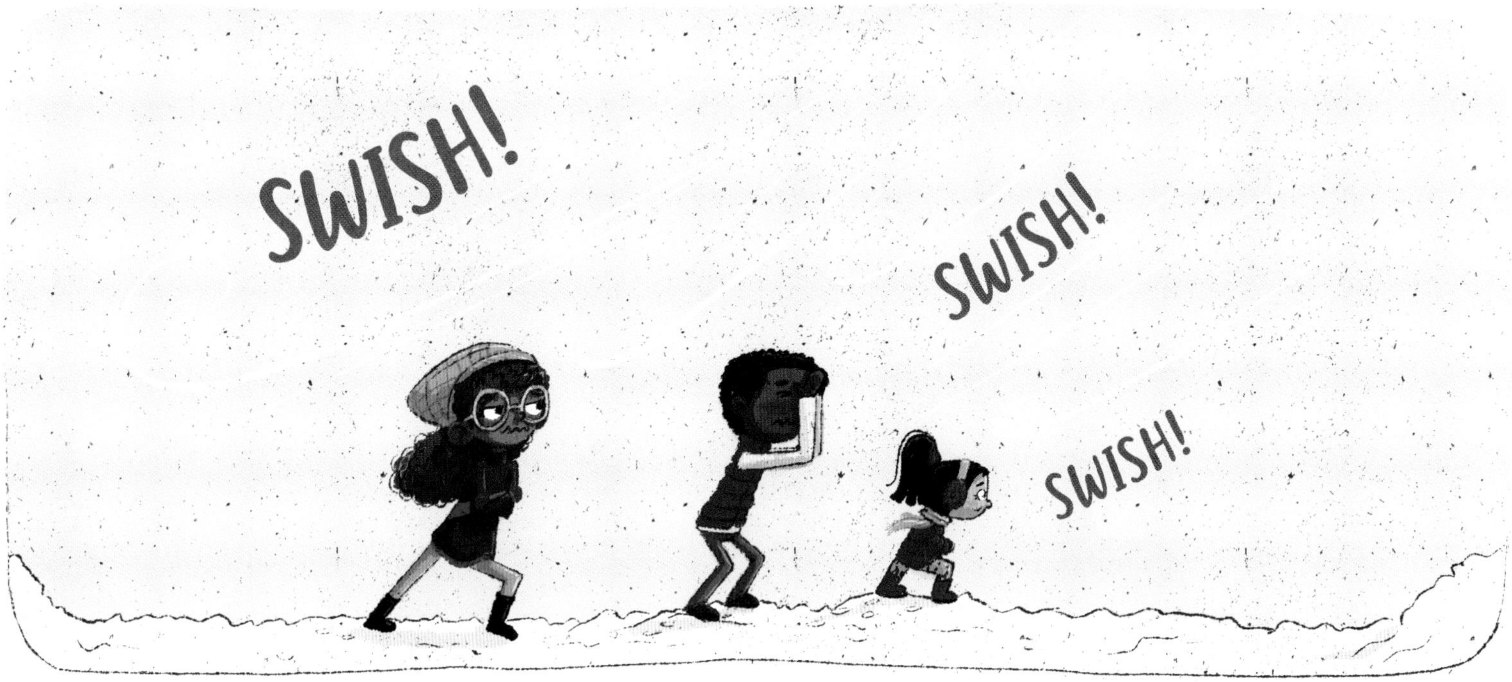
SWISH!
SWISH!
SWISH!

Get to our front door.

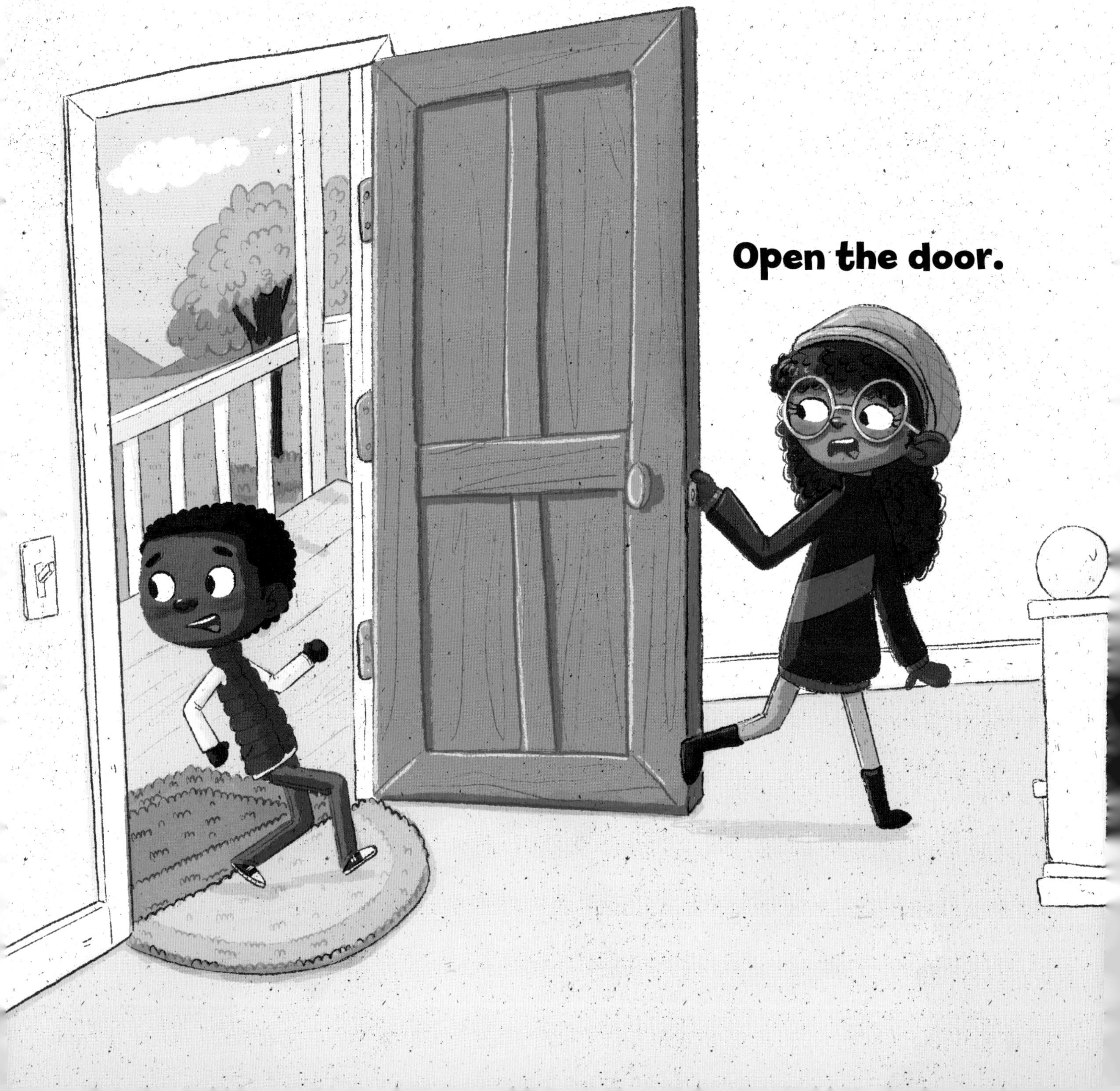

Open the door.

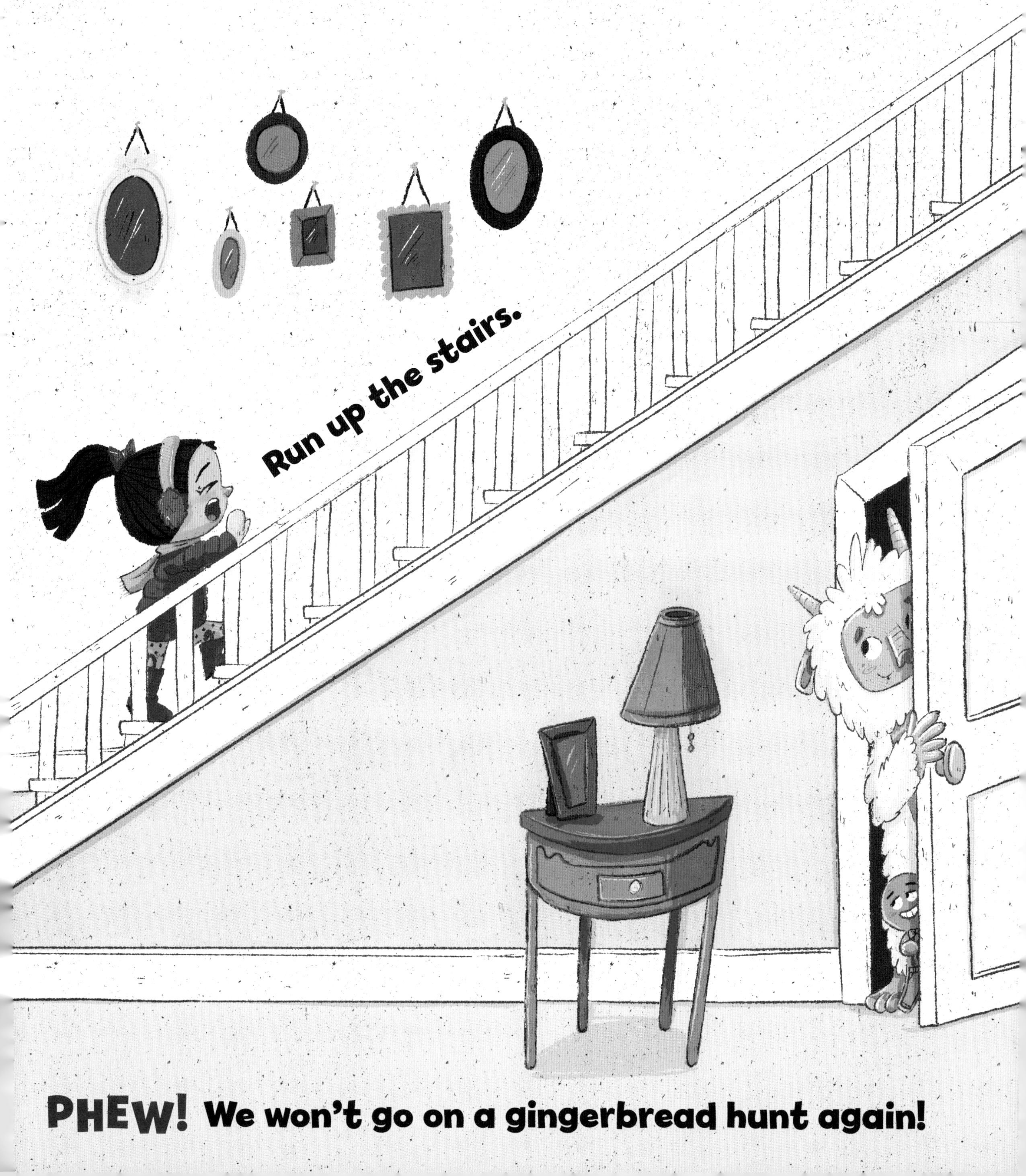

Run up the stairs.

PHEW! We won't go on a gingerbread hunt again!

For Miranda. — G.J.

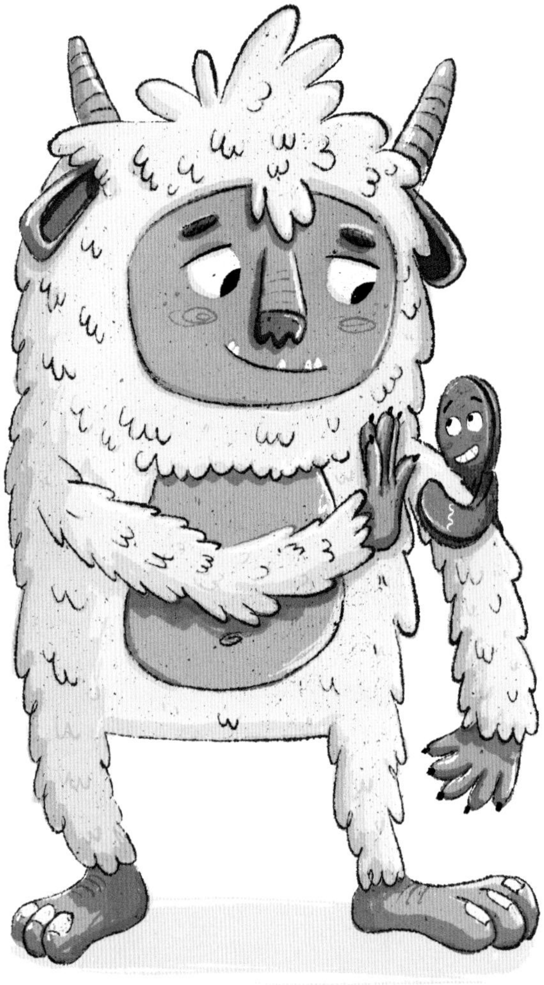

Published by Scholastic Inc., *Publishers since 1920.* SCHOLASTIC, CARTWHEEL BOOKS, and associated logos are trademarks and/or registered trademarks of Scholastic Inc. • The publisher does not have any control over and does not assume any responsibility for author or third-party websites or their content. • Library of Congress Cataloging-in-Publication Data available • ISBN 978-1-338-66627-4
10 9 8 7 6 5 4 3 2 1 24 25 26 27 28 • Printed in China 38 • First edition, September 2024 • The text type was set in Palatino • The display type was set in Billy • Gladys Jose's illustrations were created using Adobe Photoshop
Designed by Rae Crawford